For further information on Enid Blyton
please contact www.blyton.com

ISBN 0-86163-996-0

First published 1952 by Brockhampton Press Limited in
Enid Blyton's Bright Story Book
This edition first published 1984
Re-issued 1999

Published by Award Publications Limited,
27 Longford Street, London NW1 3DZ

Printed in India

Enid Blyton

THEY CAN'T CATCH BRER RABBIT

Illustrated by Suzy-Jane Tanner

AWARD PUBLICATIONS LIMITED

"You know," said Brer Fox to Brer Wolf, "it's just about time we caught Brer Rabbit, Brer Wolf. He's getting so uppity these days, he'll soon be ordering us about!"

"Well, let's catch him, then," said Brer Wolf. "We'll think of a plan. Shall we set a trap for him?"

"I've got a better idea than that," said Brer Fox. "We'll catch him in a net!"

"How can we do that?" said Brer Wolf. "He'll see a net."

"Now, you listen," said Brer Fox. "We'll have a hunting party, see? You can bring a net to catch butterflies and I'll bring one to catch fish. And we'll tell Brer Rabbit to bring a net, too, and catch what he likes. We'll say that we'll bring the lunch; he needn't bother to bring any."

"And when he's not looking, we'll clap our nets down over him and that will be the end of old Brer Rabbit!" said Brer Wolf, pleased. "A mighty fine idea, Brer Fox!"

Well, the two of them told Brer Rabbit about their hunting party and Brer Rabbit listened carefully with both of his long ears.

"You bring your net and catch what you like," said Brer Fox. "We'll bring ours, too. And don't you bother about any food, Brer Rabbit; we'll bring that and we'll share it with you."

"Well, that's mighty kind of you," said Brer Rabbit. "I'll be pleased to come. And don't forget I like carrot sandwiches, will you?"

Now, when the day for the hunting party came, Brer Rabbit made up his mind he'd go along to the meeting place quite early. It seemed a bit funny that Brer Fox and Brer Wolf should be so friendly with him all of a sudden. So off he went early and crawled under a bush to wait for the other two, taking his net with him.

Presently, along came Brer Fox and Brer Wolf, each with the most enormous net.

"Heyo, Brer Fox!" said Brer Wolf. "My, you ought to catch old Brer Rabbit in that! That net of yours is big enough to catch an elephant."

"And yours is strong enough to catch a tiger!" said Brer Fox. "Now, we must each pretend to be looking for fish or for butterflies as soon as we see old Brer Rabbit coming. You wait about by those flowers and I'll sit down at the stream here. He's late."

"Oho!" thought Brer Rabbit to himself. "I'm late, am I? It's a good thing I was early, it seems to me!"

"Did you bring a picnic lunch?" called Brer Wolf to Brer Fox.

"Yes. I'll put it down here," shouted back Brer Fox, and he put down a nice large basket of food not far from Brer Rabbit's bush. The smell of it reached Brer Rabbit's nose and it was very good.

Brer Wolf danced about among the flowers with his net and Brer Fox swished about in the stream with his. They both kept an eye open for Brer Rabbit, but he didn't come, and he didn't come.

Brer Rabbit was looking through a hole in his bush at that picnic basket and wishing he could feast on what was inside it.

He waited till Brer Fox
and Brer Wolf were
looking the other way –
and then he quietly
pushed his net out from
under the bush and put it
over the basket.

He began to draw it carefully back towards the bush.
He soon got it under the bush and opened the basket.
My, how good everything smelled!

"I'll take it home to my family!" thought Brer Rabbit.
"That's what I'll do!"

So, as bold as brass, he crept out from under the bush and shouted to Brer Fox and Brer Wolf.

"Heyo, folks! Having a nice party? I hope you'll catch what you went to catch!"

Brer Fox almost fell into the stream when he heard Brer Rabbit shout. Brer Wolf stepped into some nettles and then stepped out again in a hurry.

"Where did you come from?" shouted Brer Fox. "We've been watching out for you for a long time. We wanted you to go hunting with us. You come here and see what I've caught."

"I've been hunting under that bush," said Brer Rabbit. "You wouldn't believe what I caught!"

He swung his net round and Brer Fox suddenly saw that Brer Rabbit had got his picnic basket in it. He gave an angry yell and rushed at him. Brer Rabbit danced away.

"You're a thief, Brer Rabbit!" cried Brer Fox.

"Yes, that's what you are!"
agreed Brer Wolf. "You just
came to steal our lunch.
You didn't come here to
catch anything."

"I did, I did!" shouted Brer Rabbit, dancing round and
round a bush and making Brer Fox come after him with
his net.

"Well, you tell me what you came to catch, then!" yelled Brer Fox. "You just tell me."

Brer Rabbit ran to the hedge and waved his net at Brer Fox. "You go and catch fish, Brer Fox, and leave me to catch what I want to catch."

"What are you going to catch? You tell me that!" shouted Brer Fox.

Brer Rabbit leaped right over the hedge. A bus was rumbling up the lane. Brer Rabbit put out his hand and stopped it.

"Heyo, Brer Fox!" he called, as he hopped on to the step. "I'm catching the bus. That's what I'm catching. The bus!" And off he went with the picnic basket in his net, laughing so much he could hardly put his hand into his pocket for the fare!